For George and Zoë

Henry Holt and Company, LLC

Publishers since 1866

115 West 18th Street, New York, New York 10011

www.henryholt.com

Henry Holt is a registered trademark of Henry Holt and Company, LLC

Copyright © 2003 by Leslie Baker. All rights reserved.

Distributed in Canada by H. B. Fenn and Company Ltd.

Library of Congress Cataloging-in-Publication Data

Baker, Leslie A. The animal ABC / Leslie Baker.

Summary: Labeled illustrations present a different animal for each letter
of the alphabet, from ant and iguana to quail and zebra.

1. Animals—Juvenile literature. 2. English language—Alphabet—Juvenile literature.
[1. Animals. 2. Alphabet.] I. Title. QL49.B143 2003   590—dc21   2002004360

ISBN 0-8050-6746-9 / First Edition—2003 / Designed by Donna Mark

Printed in the United States of America on acid-free paper. ∞

1 3 5 7 9 10 8 6 4 2

The artist used watercolor on Montval paper to create the illustrations for this book.

The Animal ABC

Leslie Baker

HENRY HOLT AND COMPANY • NEW YORK

Aa

Ant

Bb

Bear

Cc

Chimpanzee

Dd

Dog

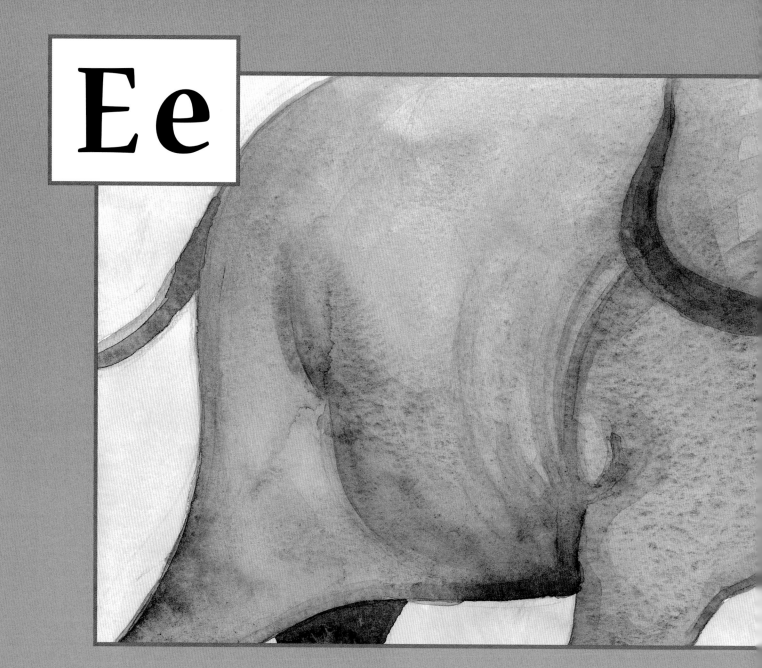

Ee

Elephant

F f

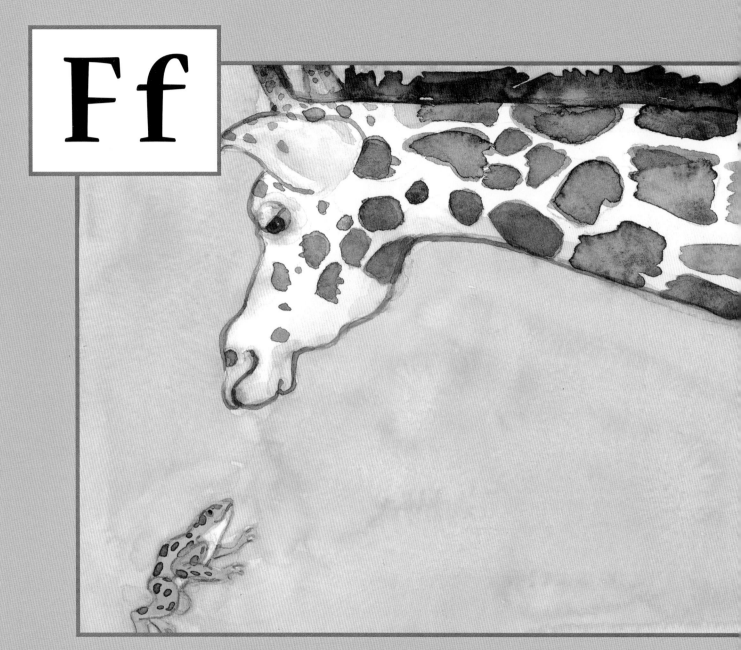

Frog

Gg

Giraffe

Hh

Horse

I i

Iguana

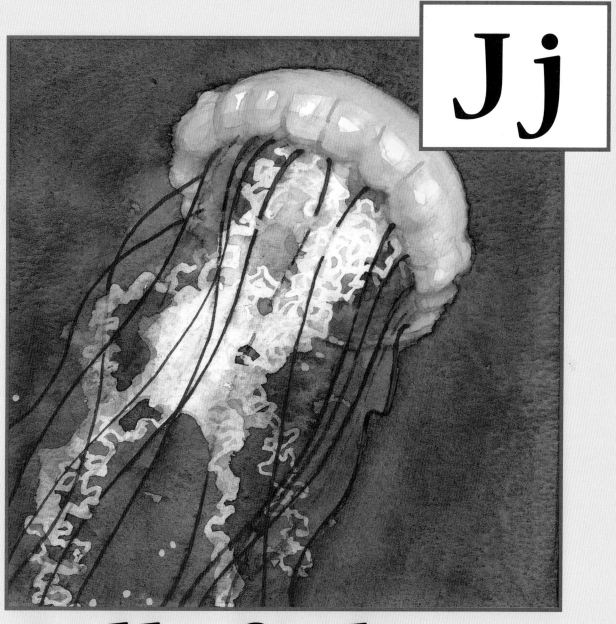

J j

Jellyfish

Kk

Koala

L l

Lobster

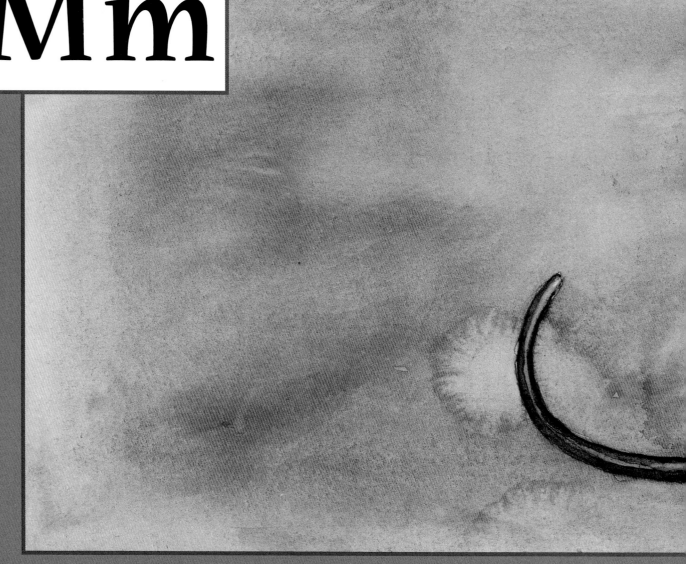

Mm

Mouse

Nn

Nuthatch

Oo

Opossum

Pp

Panda

Qq

Quail

Rr

Raccoon

Ss

Spider

Tt

Tiger

Uu

Uakari

Vv

Vole

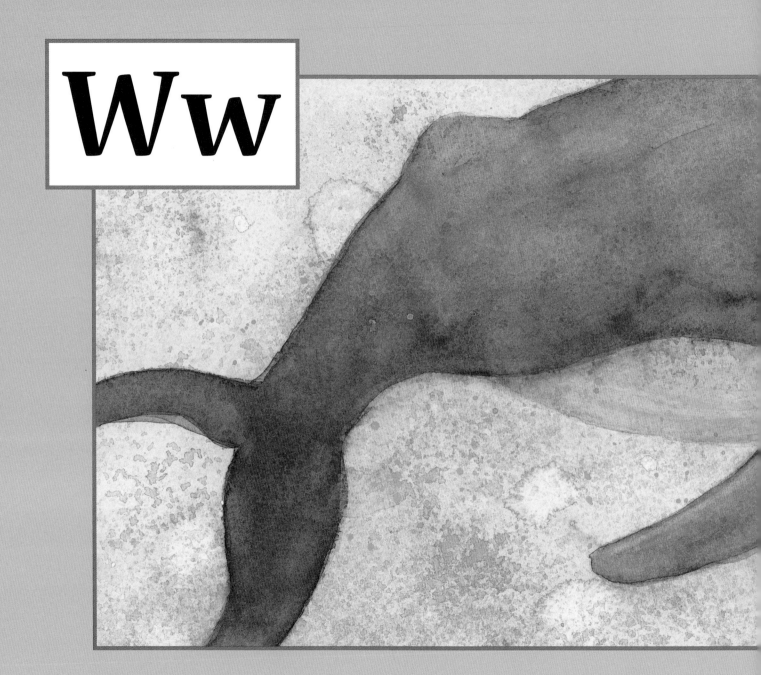

W w

Whale

Xx

oX

Yy

Yellowtail

Zz

Zebra

A	a	B	b	C	c	D	d	E
J	j	K	k	L	l	M	m	N
S	S	T	t	U	u	V	v	W
B	b	C	c	D	d	E	e	F
K	k	L	l	M	m	N	n	O
T	t	U	u	V	v	W	w	X
C	c	D	d	E	e	F	f	G
L	l	M	m	N	n	O	o	P
U	u	V	v	W	w	X	x	Y